# Quack!

St. Clare of Montefalco School

Written by Matthew Benjamin
Illustrated by Kristen Goeters

Three little ducks,
one, two, three.

2

Quick, little ducks,
swim here to me.

3

Three little ducks
as quiet as can be.

Quick, little ducks,
swim here to me.

Three quick ducks
all swimming back.

Quack, quack, quack, quack,
quack, quack, quack!

Three little ducks, one, two, three.

8   Quick, little ducks, swim here to me.